The Twinniest Twins

written by Amy Kuhr
illustrated by Natayla Pilavci

Dillsburg Area Public Library

204 Mumper Lane
Dillsburg, PA 17019

to my sweet Little Man
and my Little Miss

you have brought me more laughter
and love than I knew was possible

4171 Crescent Dr., Ste. 101-A, St. Louis, MO 63129
or visit them on the Internet at:
www.sbgpublishing.com
ISBN 978-1-941434-66-6
Text copyright© 2017 by Amy Kuhr
Illustrations copyright© 2017 by Amy Kuhr
All rights reserved.
Published by StoryBook Genius, LLC.
Printed in the U.S.A.

StoryBook Genius Publishing
SbgPublishing.com

expanding minds
opening hearts
igniting curiosity

Book design
that makes you
go yippee!
yipjar.com

I am Trent.

I am Morgan.

She's my twin sister...

...he's my twin brother...

and everyday, we have fun with each other!

We love to play outside.

I love to walk!

I love to ride!

We love to jump,
so we both do!

We may be different,
but we are twins,
TOO!

Yet — we are twins.
The twinniest that
twins can BE!

I read my book...

...while I watch tv.

Yet – we are twins.
The twinniest that
twins can BE!

We both l♡ve to take baths

and to build

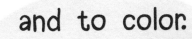

and to color.

We swing

we sing

we dance
with each other.

Yet - we are very different
like every sister and brother!

I love my bunny...

...I love my monkey

...but we both make mommy laugh
and she says we're both funny!

I love to climb...

...and
I love
to throw

Dillsburg Area Public Library

204 Mumper Lane
Dillsburg, PA 17019

...but we are both happy
when we're on the go!

People say that we look the same, but we always explain...

We are different but one thing is the same—

the love that we share as
twin sister and brother.

So if you are twins
and you don't look alike,

or even if you
have a big fight

— that's okay!

It's great to be you!

Because just like us...
you're twins, **TOO!**

CPSIA information can be obtained at www.ICGtesting.com
Printed in the USA
BVIW12n2006160717
489262BV00008B/127